Robyn Smythe was born in 1967 in Fife, Scotland, and was educated at Madras College Secondary school where he went from 1979 to 1985.

In his younger days, he had visions of joining the police, but fate intervened and instead he has had two quite contrasting jobs since leaving school – working behind the counter in the Post Office and being a lifeguard at the local pool.

He is married with two teenage girls and his hobbies include watching movies, walking, and swimming. Writing has always been a passion for him. He wrote his first full-length story back in secondary school, as an English assignment, but he never had the time or inclination to pursue it until the whole world went into lockdown with Covid-19.

A CIP catalogue record for this title is available from the British Library.

ISBN 9781398472754 (Paperback)
ISBN 9781398472761 (ePub e-book)

www.austinmacauley.com

First Published 2022
Austin Macauley Publishers Ltd®
1 Canada Square
Canary Wharf
London
E14 5AA

This book is dedicated to Maria, a dear friend and colleague who relit the fire within me to become a writer. Our conversations energised me to succeed.

""Bedtime, young lady."

"But 'Pops'!" She protested.

"The sandman waits for no man or little girl. Come on, up you go." He scooped her up in his mighty arms and carried her upstairs to her room. He plonked her down gently outside her door and signalled with his hand for her to go in. She smiled a broad smile and went in, then paused, looking back to see him still standing in the doorway. "A gentleman never sees a young lady undress." He explained quietly shut the door. "Ready." Molly announced as she propped herself up in bed with the help of two massive pillows. The door opened and 'Pops' came in carrying a mug of steaming liquid. Hot chocolate. Yum! Thought Molly as she took the warm mug in both hands. She carefully put it on her bedside table. "I'll have that a little later. It's just a tad too hot." That smile from 'Pops' again as he allowed her to snuggle down before he tucked her in like a miniature caterpillar in its cocoon.

"Good night, my little adventurer." Said the old man as he went towards the door.

"Good night, my old adventurer". The old man turned one final time to check on her before switching off the

light, closing the door and heading downstairs. Molly snuggled deeply into the pillows, allowing them to engulf her in a soft feathery embarrass. It did not take long for her to drop off to sleep.

Meanwhile, downstairs in the study, Grandpa was sitting at his desk puffing on his pipe thoughtfully. He liked having his granddaughter staying, even if it was in uncertain times. She brought life back to both him and the house. He reached over to a drawer with his left hand and opened it. He took out a photograph in a silver frame and sat it in front of him. He lent back in his chair that creaked under the strain to get a better look at the picture. It showed a single female, roughly in her twenties, wearing what looked like a light summery dress and a straw wide brimmed hat over dark coloured shoulder length hair. The dress hugged her slim figure exaggerating every curve. Grandpa found himself drifting back through the mists of time to when the picture was taken.

A sudden crack of thunder and a child screaming brough 'Pops' back to the present. He rushed upstairs to find Molly bolt upright in her bed sobbing. He seemed to glide across the floor to her beside and wrapped his arms around her. He rubbed the middle of her back as he whispered in her ear that it was nothing to be afraid

of and she was perfectly safe. She pulled back and looked into his eyes, tears streaming down her face. He smiled that soothing smile he had as she scooped her up once more and took her downstairs. He gently sat her down in one of the huge leather armchairs, placed a blanket over her from the waist down and then sat across from her. Fear still etched on her face.

"Now, my little adventurer, this will not do." He scolded but with a smile on his face that was infectious as the fear disappeared like the early morning mist. "The thunder is only the Moon's stomach rumbling because he, unlike you, hasn't had his hot chocolate and toast for his supper." A faint smile appeared on Molly's face.   CRACK! The thunder sounded and the little girl jumped nearly three feet up in the air. An impressive achievement an Olympic Gold Medallist would have been proud of from a standing start. The tears started to fall again down her cheeks like little rivers and her face became twisted like it was melting. Then a strange noise came from her mouth. A cross between a wail and a scream. As if someone had trodden on one of those squeaky toys and the squeaker had shot across the floor. 'Pops' froze for a moment. In his head wondering if children of this age came with either an off switch or mute button and where would such a device be located. FLASH! Went the lightning. Even 'Pops' was caught

off guard by that and he jumped but not as high as he was old and creaky. He fanned himself with his hand and pretended to faint. Molly's orchestral melt down paused as she looked at the puzzling antics of her relative. Then she laughed and laughed and laughed and…..I think you get the idea. 'Pops' opened one eye and squinted across at the youngster who was now rolling about the floor. He too found the affair hilarious and decided to join in with the rolling and the laughing. After a few minutes of complete silliness, 'Pops' got to his feet and composed himself by clearing his throat.

"The lightning really scares me, Pops." Said Molly looking up at him.

"Now! Now!" He began his mind racing to try and give her a reasonable explanation. "The lightning is just God taking a picture with the new camera Missus God gave him on his birthday. God has simply forgotten to switch the flash bulb off." Amazing what an adult's brain can come up with in an emergency, huh? "Perhaps, a story will help." He said as he crossed his legs, made himself comfortable and reached into the breast pocket of his waistcoat and pulled out a pair of half-moon spectacles and put them on hooking them on behind his ears. .
One of her Grandpa's greatest gifts was his story telling. Molly thought it was something to do with all the travels

and adventures he had had. He always managed
to dream up some new adventure for ever visit with a
Grandpa or 'Pops' twist.

"Now, this story was told to me by a local tribal chief
who swore to me that it was true. Are you sitting
comfortably?" Molly nodded as she cradled her mug of
steaming liquid in both hands. "Then I will begin."

*'Deep in the jungle in deepest Africa is held a gathering
not seen by humans. The animals have a tea party
and at this tea party an amazing thing happens – the
animals begin talk like you and me. How do I know this?
I was told by a passing giraffe one day while I was out
sunbathing in the noon day sun without a hat or any
shade. The moral being – too much sun and not enough
water to drink and the animals might start talking to you.*

At the end of every month with a letter of the alphabet in it, at twilight when the sun clocks out and the moon clocks in, an invitation goes out on the jungle drums (this story takes place before the invention of the jungle telegraph) for certain animals to gather in the clearing. If a human was to hear the message it would sound like –Boom! Titty! Boom! Titty! Boom! – which you would agree sounds like a very bad percussion session but the animals know what it means. The food on display was fit for jungle royalty. There was roasted beetle cake, sirloin of zebra, dung beetle moose, hyena flapjacks (not made of but made by Horace the Hyena, a gourmet chef and part time stand–up comic), there was of course tea (brewed to perfection in a camels mouth before it was spat out into the teapot and hot water added) and there was a selection of cheeses for Mike, who squeaked.

Invited this month was Lionel the Lion, Tabitha the Toucan, Terrence the Turtle, Ally the Alligator, Colin the Crocodile, the Pelican and Mike the Mouse. Lionel always got invited because it was royal protocol with him being the king of the jungle and so vain it is unreal.

It takes him four hours just to get the curlers in his mane, blow dried and set. His invitation when out last week. Lionel was always accompanied by Maurice the Gorilla, his bodyguard or muscle as Lionel refers to him as. Now poor Maurice always stayed four steps behind his royalness, with his large hairy arms folded across his chest, for two reasons. Firstly, it was the done, thing when you were part of the royal protection squad, that was obvious. The second reason was a more personal one – Maurice had a delicate stomach and one of the more embarrassing side effects of this was a bad case of wind. Maurice was also allergic to bananas which did cause difficulties on pay day because that was the main currency for the job that he did. "They don't grow on trees you know." Lionel was once heard to exclaim. "

Please, dearest Molly, before you interrupt or correct me, I am aware that bananas grow on trees but Lionel is the King of the Jungle and it's very dangerous to correct him. Also, please don't tell Maurice you know about his rather 'smelly' issue because he is liable to go ape!

Tabitha the toucan likes to do two things. Talking and be centre of attention. She is also from a well to do nest, posh in other words, and looks down her beak at everyone which, going by the size of it is the only thing she can do.

She takes great pride in her appearance constantly preening herself keeping her jet black body in tip-top condition. Her latest issue she has going on was if her beak was bright enough as she had read in 'Feather your Nest' magazine (the go-to publication for those birds on the social perch) that as toucans get older, the colour in their beaks tend to fade and wondering if she should get a bill enhancement procedure done to bring out the colour a bit more. The rest of the animals agreed from behind sunglasses mainly for the Peace and quiet that came with her thinking if she was doing the right thing or not.

Now you may be wondering how the animals could see with the fact that the moon was out and to make things worse, he had decided to go eco-friendly for the next month which meant the light he was giving out was at reduced power. Well, the animals had this sorted. They used fireflies. Why? Because they shine a light out of their bottoms and the animals pay the flies to buzz about thus giving them the light they need. There is one draw-back, however. Drawback is maybe the wrong word to use. Clause would be better as in clause in their contract as written out and agreed by the fireflies union. They must get ten minutes out of every hour to go down to the waterhole and cool the bottoms otherwise they are liable to overheat and in some cases, catch fire! Believe me, it's not a pretty sight seeing a firefly crash and burn.

Terence the Turtle was a championship swimmer and the only reason he was at the gathering was as a perk to teaching his royalness how to swim. Terence is also one of the most boring people you could ever have the unfortunate pleasure to meet. Get him talking about his swimming career and you get a terrible sinking feeling in your stomach. Terence comes complete already kitted out with a yellow rubber swim cap on his head with a duck on it and swimming goggles with green lenses – the colour of the lenses help him concentrate underwater, or so he told anybody that would listen.

Mike the mouse who squeaks a lot and has been hired as a background animal. The Pelican raised a white feathered wing. "Excuse me." He said but got ignored. We finally get to our star guests – no not his royalness and Maurice but Colin the Crocodile and Ally the Alligator. A first sight, these two top of the line predators look the same but you would be wrong. Ally is a few feet longer, with a long broad snout (the result of an unfortunate accident) and is also Australian (but that's not his fault). Colin is long and streamlined with a long pointed snout and he speaks with a bit of a lisp. They are lounging in a nice cool pool on the outskirts of the party sipping iced tea with little fingers raised of course. That would be unthinkable. Who do you think they were, animals?

"Ally."

"Yes."

"What's your day been like?"

"A bit snappy. The waterhole's been really busy today
with the new migration of wildebeest. Hardly had time
to set out my picnic stuff before they were on us."

"Shocking. These prey animals have no respect for
the etiquette of the hunt these days. When I was a
hatchling, my mother used to tell me that the zebra used
to wait in line to cross the river. Nowadays they just
jump in and go for it!"

" Never mind, mate. Had a bit of fun though.

""How."

"While I was in the shallows waiting for the next wave
of wildebeest, I spotted a group of human by the river
bank filming the event for some background footage for
a movie starring someone called Tarzan." Ally smiled a
long toothy smile. Now, dear Molly, a point of note. The
wildebeest is the posh name from the gnu. An animal

that can run like a cheetah but is as grumpy as a hippo. Anyway, who wants to know about an animal with a name that sounds like pooh?

"You didn't!"

"I did mate! I submerged under the water and got as close as I could before launching myself out of the water. I fell short of the humans but you should have seen them drop their equipment and run!" He gave out a snigger.

Now you must understand, dearest reader, that when either a crocodile or an alligator sniggers, it is like someone putting a pebble in a drain pipe and shaking it.

"One of them even smelt a bit like old Maurice over there but he wasn't half walking funny like an ostrich with piles!" Colin now sniggered in fact that quickly changed to a huge belly laugh, an infectious one because Ally was soon rolling over and over like he was doing his famous death roll impression.

The pelican raise a white feathered wing. "Excuse me." He got ignored. Mike the mouse went squeak.

"How was your day Colin?"

"Relaxing. I lay about the sand bank opening my mouth now and again to cool down and scare the tourists. I can't cope with this heat you know. My skin dries out and gets all leathery and tough. It costs me a fortune in sun screen and moisturiser you know."

I know, dear reader, that alligator and crocodile skin is tough and scaly but do you have the heart to tell him?
"I came across the body of a hippo today." Continued Colin, " it was Hazel…"

"Hazel the hippo? The one that was going on all those crazy diets?"

"Yip. Boy, had she let herself go! The fat was just dropping off her. Just had enough time to have her for lunch before I had to come here hence the reason I'm not eating much."

"Crikey mate! That answers that question. I thought you were off your food."

The pelican raised a white feathery wing. "Excuse me." He was ignored. Mike squeaked and ate a piece of cheese.

His royalness got to his feet and regally sauntered across to the table. With one flick of his lionicured (the same as manicured but for big cats, the posh and regal way to keep one's claws looking spectacular unlike the peasants who had to use the scratching tree down by the watering hole) claw swallowed a whole sirloin of zebra. Flick and it was done with a slight twinkle from his teeth that had been whitened at great expense the day

before. He regally sauntered back to his chair and re-joined the conversation the Terence. Lionel yawned that gave him the look of the lion from that film studio, M.G.M. Lionel always wondered whether that lion was roaring or yawning with boredom as he was."

Here, I can insert a little known fact, dearest Molly. I bet you did not know that Lionel actually had got the part of the M.G.M lion in his younger days but he was so vain. In fact, he spent so much time flossing and brushing his teeth they had to go with his stand in and the stand in got fed up waiting upon Lionel, hence the yawn. The head of the studio liked it so much, they decided to keep it.

"Both Terence and Tabitha were going great guns telling anyone within earshot about their lives. Maurice pardoned himself as his left hand wafted from side to side just at left bottom cheek level. His royalness' nostrils curled up with offence whilst Terence's goggle steamed up and he hurriedly reach for a nose clip. Even Tabitha's eyes were watering which made her make-up run like small rivers down her cheeks.

The pelican raised a white feathered wing and said, "Excuse me."

"What is it?" Came the joint reply from everyone at the party finally letting into the annoyance.

"Is this the green room for the cast of 'African Queen' as I'm an extra in the movie and it's my first day?"

"No, it isn't mate." Said Ally from the pool. "Next clearing across." He pointed roughly in that direction with a lazy claw.

"Thank you." And with two mighty downward beats from his wings, the pelican was gone.

"Who was that guy, mate?" He asked Colin who shrugged his shoulders and sipped on his tea.

His royalness got to his feet again, whispered something in Terence's ear and moved off into the jungle. That was the signal for the end of this month's tea party. Tabitha had managed to touch up her makeup and she silently (which was against character) flew off.

Mike the mouse did not squeak anymore because he had become an after party snack for his royalness who scooped him just before he disappeared back into the jungle.

"Ally?" Began Colin as they climbed out of the pool and started to walk, as crocodiles and alligators do, foot forward, tail swish, foot forward, tail swish.
"What mate?"

"Something's been bugging me since we became friends."

"What is it, mate?"

"Why is your snout flat and broad and mine is long and thin?"

"Good question mate. It's because when I was a little nipper an elephant came into the waterhole where I was and decided to sit in the water and bathe. The stupid animal was not looking where she was going and sat on me!"'

Molly gave out a huge yawn that would have challenged the M.G.M lion and did a huge stretch that turned her into a four legged spider, a cut price spider if you wish. The sandman had finally caught up with the little girl. Her grandpa beamed a contented smile and scouped her up in his big strong arms. She put her arms around his neck and snuggled in as he carried her out of the study and back up the stairs. The storm still raged outside but Molly knew know that, as long as her Grandpa was there, nothing could harm her.

She felt safe and was safe.

"Good night, my little adventurer." Whispered the old man again as he went towards the door.

"Good night, my old adventurer". Came the muffled replied from somewhere under the covers. The old man turned one final time to check on her before switching off the light, closing the door and heading downstairs.

The above story was told to nine year old Molly by her grandfather Jonathan Fallon during a thunderstorm in the novel 'Fallon – Non Est Optio Defectum' by Robyn Smythe